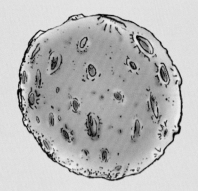

The Baboon who Went to the Moon
A Storytime Africa Book
ISBN 978 - 0 - 620 - 36181 - 1

First published in the Republic of South Africa, in 2006 by
Storytime Africa, 1 Third Avenue, Fish Hoek 7975.

Storytime Africa cc Reg. No. 2001/055268/23

Printed in South Africa in 2006
Reprinted in 2009, 2012 and 2015

www.storytimeafrica.com

THE BABOON WHO WENT TO THE MOON

John Bush
and JC Phillips

One night, when the moon shone full in the sky,

Baboon tried to jump there, he jumped so high,
But the moon is as high as high can be,
So Baboon went and found the tallest tree.

He climbed... and he climbed...
and he climbed... and he climbed,
Till he reached the top, only to find,
That the tallest tree wasn't tall enough.
'There must be a way!' he said in a huff.

He bent a strong branch into a bow,
And fired himself at the moon like an arrow.
High in the sky that giant bow shot him.
Slowly but surely, gravity got him.

Slowly but surely, that force turned him round
And he hurtled back headlong into the ground.
He dug himself out and scratched his head,
'Methinks I need more speed,' he said.

He crept up quietly on Elephant sleeping,
Put his lips to her ear, then began shrieking.

Poor Elephant trumpeted, 'Get lost, Baboon!'
And hurled him away, 'Go live on the moon!'
'Yahoo!' yelled Baboon, 'You've made my day!
Moon here I come! I'm on my way!'

This time Baboon soared upwards for longer.
An elephant's strong but gravity's stronger.
He splashed to earth in a cool, clear fountain.
Refreshed, he set off for a sky-high mountain.

Up Baboon scuttled. He reached the peak soon.
But **still** he was far, far away from the moon.

He made a magnificent, super-sized kite,
Complete with a port and starboard light.

The wind swept him up but, alas, went to rest.
What happened next, I am sure you will guess!

He decided to fashion a hot-air balloon,
Hoping he'd float right up to the moon.
But the fire he made to lift the craft up,
Burnt it to cinders. What rotten luck!

Then he begged two vultures, snoring nearby,
'Please measure how far to the moon on high.'

'Baboon you're crazy!' they squawked in dismay.
'Not even vultures can fly the whole way!'

So he went to town, played a game of cricket,
And booked himself a night flight ticket.

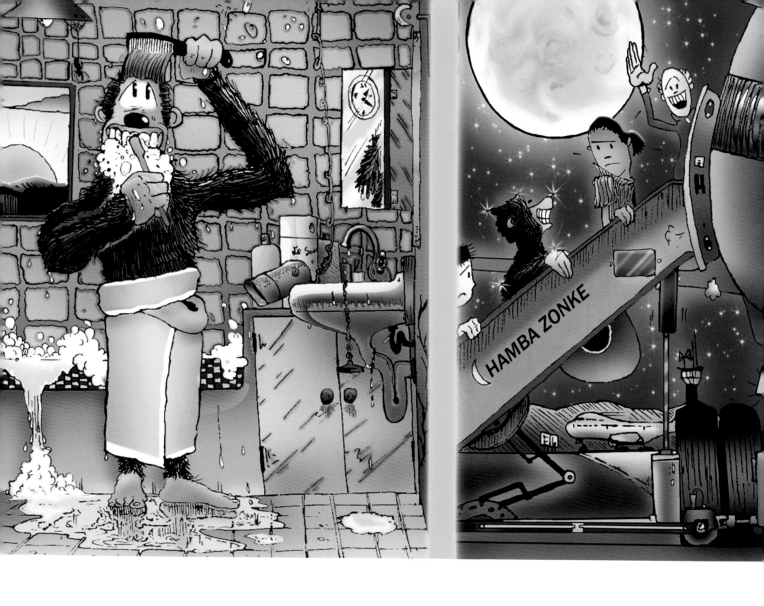

He brushed his teeth and combed his hair
To look his best on arriving there.

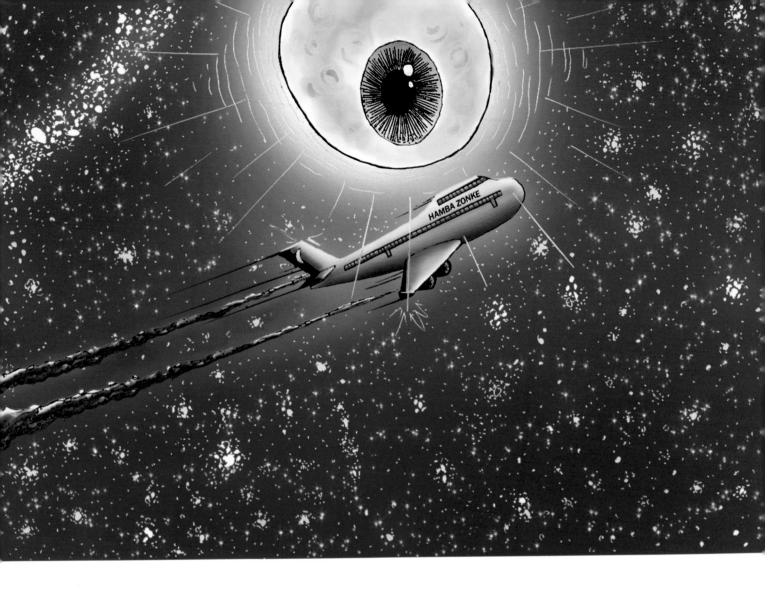

As the jet soared up in the dark night sky,
The moon looked down like a big yellow eye.

He asked the hostess, dressed in maroon,
'When do we get to the big yellow moon?'
'The big yellow moon? Good gracious, Baboon!
This flight only goes to Potchefstroom!'

Dejected and sad and out of pocket,
He went back home and built his own rocket;

An amazing machine, a massive missile.
'I'll get there now,' he said with a smile.

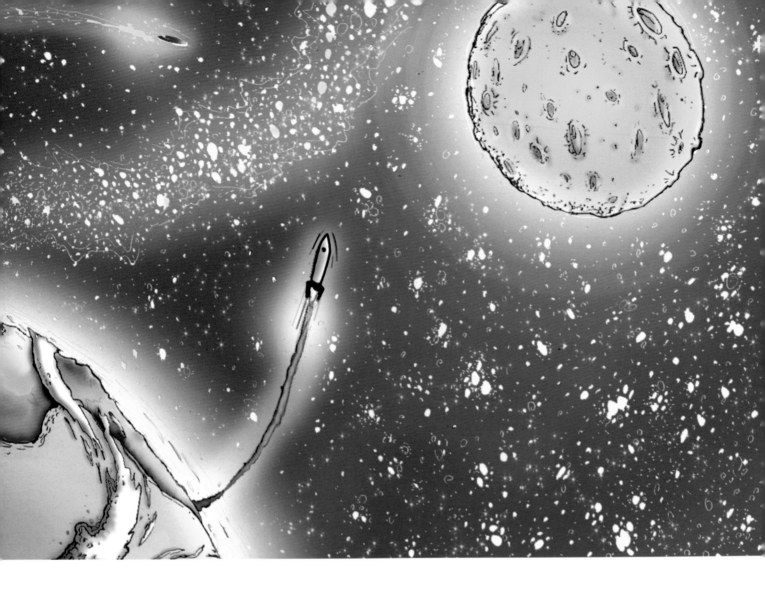

And he did, you know, one star-swept night,
As the moon shone full and round and bright.

He played in the moon dust for all he was worth.
He jumped far higher than he could on earth.

He met a whole tribe of green, moon baboons,
Who had seven legs and fingers like spoons.
He built himself a little moon shack
And made up his mind he'd **never** come back.

Baboon was as happy as happy can be,
Till one fine night, he happened to see
A twinkle of red amidst the stars.

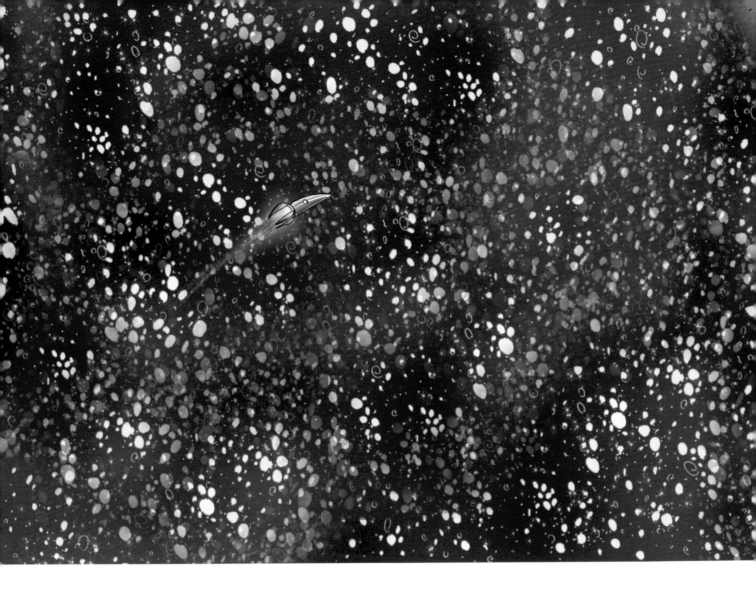

'I wonder,' he said...

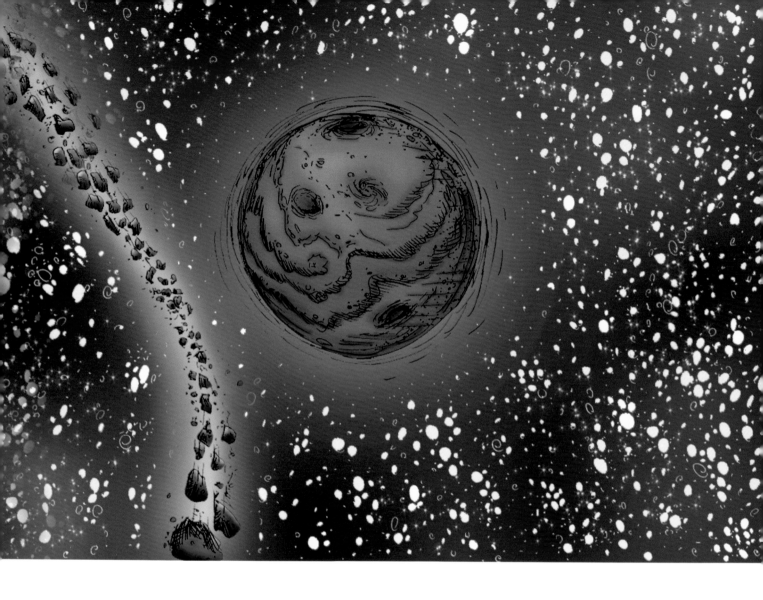

... 'what life's like on Mars?'

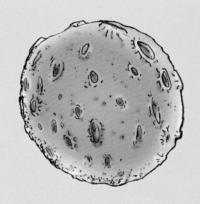

**Bestselling storyrhymes
by John Bush**

www.storytimeafrica.com